THE
MAN WHO
PLANTED
TREES

THE
MAN WHO
PLANTED
TREES

JEAN GIONO

Wood Engravings by Michael McCurdy

Foreword to the Twentieth Anniversary Edition by Wangari Maathai
Afterword to the Original Edition by Norma L. Goodrich
Afterword by Andy Lipkis

CHELSEA GREEN PUBLISHING COMPANY
White River Junction, Vermont

Printed in Canada
First printing, April 2005

10 9 8 7 6 5 4 3 2 1

Printed on acid-free, recycled paper

Originally published in Vogue under the title
"The Man Who Planted Trees and Grew Happiness."
Copyright 1954 (renewed 1982) by Conde Nast Publications, Inc.

Library of Congress Cataloging-in-Publication Data
Giono, Jean, 1895-1970.
[Homme qui plantait des arbres. English]
The man who planted trees / Jean Giono ; wood engravings by Michael McCurdy ;
foreword by Wangari Maathai ; afterword by Andy Lipkis ; afterword to original
edition by Norma L. Goodrich.-- 20th anniversary ed.
p. cm.
ISBN 1-931498-72-5 (book)
ISBN 1-931498-81-4 (book and compact disc)
I. Title.
PQ2613.I57H5813 2005
843'.912--dc22
2004028997

Chelsea Green Publishing Company
Post Office Box 428
White River Junction, VT 05001
(802) 295-6300
www.chelseagreen.com

FOREWORD

to the twentieth anniversary edition

Wangari Maathai

The Man Who Planted Trees by Jean Giono is the story of a man after my own heart. Elzéard Bouffier plants trees because he can see how ruinous everything is without them. He decides to plant hundreds of thousands of trees, and slowly the community of humans and animals around him comes back to life. His village and the countryside around it thrive, and that is reward enough for this humble man.

I first became aware of the importance of trees as a little girl, when my grandmother told me that I should not collect wood from a nearby fig tree because it was a gift from God. Even though I didn't know then why fig trees were special, I later understood that the fig tree's deep roots tapped into underground streams and brought water to the surface, replenishing the land and bringing it life. Unfortunately, that indigenous wisdom, like the tree, did not survive the forces of colonialism and globalization. The pure stream where I used to play with frogspawn and tadpoles dried up, like the tree a victim of shortsighted forestry practices and the growing of cash crops.

I began to plant trees with the Green Belt Movement (GBM), an organization I founded in 1977. Rural women in Kenya had been telling me that they had to walk further and further to collect firewood for fuel. Their families were malnourished and their land was degraded. I saw that planting trees could provide these women with firewood, fruit, fodder for their livestock, and fencing for their land, and also stop soil erosion and keep streams flowing. Like the narrator of *The Man Who Planted Trees*, I saw human communities restored along with nature. This is not a mystical phenomenon; it is a fact of human existence. Human beings cannot thrive in a place where the natural environment has been degraded.

It is interesting that Elzéard Bouffier continues his work of planting trees through two world wars and that the narrator notices that people in the village become more kindly and optimistic once the trees have grown. So much conflict over the last hundred years has been about access to natural resources—to land, oil, minerals, timber, and water. In my effort to describe the linkage between good management of the environment, democratic space and peace, I have adopted a metaphor of the three-legged African stool. The three legs represent basic pillars for stable nations without which sustainable development is unattainable. By linking environment, democracy, and peace, the Norwegian Nobel Committee expanded the concept of peace and security, and validated my long-held belief that only through an equitable distribution of those resources and their sustainable use will we be able to keep the peace. I feel that, in his quiet way, Elzéard Bouffier understands that, too.

I was amused by the narrator's observation that the professionals from the Forest Service offer only "a great deal of ineffectual talk" when they come to inspect the forest that has grown up because of Elzéard Bouffier's efforts. When we women of the GBM went to the professional foresters to ask them for seedlings, we were told we weren't qualified to plant trees. Now, women have been planting things in the ground for many centuries, and I didn't think we needed a diploma to do the same with trees. So we "foresters without diplomas" planted trees much like Elzéard Bouffier did, by cultivating the seedlings and putting them in the ground. Since we started, we have planted thirty million trees throughout Kenya and expanded into other parts of Africa. The Green Belt Movement and *The Man Who Planted Trees* make a very important point: you do not need a diploma to make a difference; everyone is qualified to save the planet.

The Man Who Planted Trees is a charming story about the virtues of environmental stewardship and tireless service—both of which are very important. However, it is also a vision of the good things that happen when we care for the world around us, and take what was barren and make it green. I hope you will let the story of Elzéard Bouffier inspire you to plant trees wherever you can.

Wangari Maathai
February 2005

THE
MAN WHO
PLANTED
TREES

FOR a human character to reveal truly exceptional qualities, one must have the good fortune to be able to observe its performance over many years. If this performance is devoid of all egoism, if its guiding motive is unparalleled generosity, if it is absolutely certain that there is no thought of recompense and that, in addition, it has left its visible mark upon the earth, then there can be no mistake.

About forty years ago I was taking a long trip on foot over mountain heights quite unknown to tourists, in that ancient region where the Alps thrust down into Provence. All this, at the time I embarked upon my long walk through these deserted regions, was barren and colorless land. Nothing grew there but wild lavender.

I was crossing the area at its widest point, and after
three days' walking, found myself in the midst of unparalleled desolation. I camped near the vestiges of
an abandoned village. I had run out of water the day
before, and had to find some. These clustered houses,
although in ruins, like an old wasps' nest, suggested
that there must once have been a spring or well here.
There was indeed a spring, but it was dry. The five
or six houses, roofless, gnawed by wind and rain, the
tiny chapel with its crumbling steeple, stood about
like the houses and chapels in living villages, but all
life had vanished.

It was a fine June day, brilliant with sunlight, but over this unsheltered land, high in the sky, the wind blew with unendurable ferocity. It growled over the carcasses of the houses like a lion disturbed at its meal. I had to move my camp.

After five hours' walking I had still not found water and there was nothing to give me any hope of finding any. All about me was the same dryness, the same coarse grasses. I thought I glimpsed in the distance a small black silhouette, upright, and took it for the trunk of a solitary tree. In any case I started toward it. It was a shepherd. Thirty sheep were lying about him on the baking earth.

He gave me a drink from his water-gourd and, a little later, took me to his cottage in a fold of the plain. He drew his water—excellent water—from a very deep natural well above which he had constructed a primitive winch.

The man spoke little. This is the way of those who live alone, but one felt that he was sure of himself, and confident in his assurance. That was unexpected in this barren country. He lived, not in a cabin, but in a real house built of stone that bore plain evidence of how his own efforts had reclaimed the ruin he had found there on his arrival. His roof was strong and sound. The wind on its tiles made the sound of the sea upon its shore.

The place was in order, the dishes washed, the floor swept, his rifle oiled; his soup was boiling over the fire. I noticed then that he was cleanly shaved, that all his buttons were firmly sewed on, that his clothing had been mended with the meticulous care

that makes the mending invisible. He shared his soup with me and afterwards, when I offered my tobacco pouch, he told me that he did not smoke. His dog, as silent as himself, was friendly without being servile.

It was understood from the first that I should spend the night there; the nearest village was still more than a day and a half away. And besides I was perfectly familiar with the nature of the rare villages in that region. There were four or five of them scattered well apart from each other on these mountain slopes, among white oak thickets, at the extreme end

of the wagon roads. They were inhabited by charcoalburners, and the living was bad. Families, crowd-
ed together in a climate that is excessively harsh both
in winter and in summer, found no escape from the
unceasing conflict of personalities. Irrational ambi-
tion reached inordinate proportions in the continual
desire for escape. The men took their wagonloads
of charcoal to the town, then returned. The soundest
characters broke under the perpetual grind. The
women nursed their grievances. There was rivalry in
everything, over the price of charcoal as over a pew
in the church, over warring virtues as over warring

vices as well as over the ceaseless combat between virtue and vice. And over all there was the wind, also ceaseless, to rasp upon the nerves. There were epidemics of suicide and frequent cases of insanity, usually homicidal.

The shepherd went to fetch a small sack and poured out a heap of acorns on the table. He began to inspect them, one by one, with great concentration, separating the good from the bad. I smoked my pipe. I did offer to help him. He told me that it was his job. And in fact, seeing the care he devoted to the task, I did not insist. That was the whole of our conversation. When he had set aside a large enough pile of good acorns he counted them out by tens, meanwhile eliminating the small ones or those which were slightly cracked, for now he examined them more closely. When he had thus selected one hundred perfect acorns he stopped and we went to bed.

There was peace in being with this man. The next day I asked if I might rest here for a day. He found

it quite natural—or, to be more exact, he gave me the impression that nothing could startle him. The rest was not absolutely necessary, but I was interested and wished to know more about him. He opened the pen and led his flock to pasture. Before leaving, he plunged his sack of carefully selected and counted acorns into a pail of water.

I noticed that he carried for a stick an iron rod as thick as my thumb and about a yard and a half long. Resting myself by walking, I followed a path parallel to his. His pasture was in a valley. He left the dog in charge of the little flock and climbed toward where I stood. I was afraid that he was about to rebuke me for my indiscretion, but it was not that at all: this was the way he was going, and he invited me to go along if I had nothing better to do. He climbed to the top of the ridge, about a hundred yards away.

There he began thrusting his iron rod into the earth, making a hole in which he planted an acorn; then he refilled the hole. He was planting oak trees. I asked him if the land belonged to him. He answered no. Did he know whose it was? He did not. He supposed it was community property, or perhaps belonged to people who cared nothing about it. He was not interested in finding out whose it was. He planted his hundred acorns with the greatest care.

After the midday meal he resumed his planting. I suppose I must have been fairly insistent in my questioning, for he answered me. For three years he had been planting trees in this wilderness. He had planted one hundred thousand. Of the hundred thousand, twenty thousand had sprouted. Of the twenty thousand he still expected to lose about half, to rodents or to the unpredictable designs of Providence. There remained ten thousand oak trees to grow where nothing had grown before.

That was when I began to wonder about the age of this man. He was obviously over fifty. Fifty-five, he told me. His name was Elzéard Bouffier. He had once had a farm in the lowlands. There he had had his life. He had lost his only son, then his wife. He had withdrawn into this solitude where his pleasure was to live leisurely with his lambs and his dog. It was his opinion that this land was dying for want of trees. He added that, having no very pressing busi-

ness of his own, he had resolved to remedy this state of affairs.

Since I was at that time, in spite of my youth, leading a solitary life, I understood how to deal gently with solitary spirits. But my very youth forced me to consider the future in relation to myself and to a certain quest for happiness. I told him that in thirty years his ten thousand oaks would be magnificent. He answered quite simply that if God granted him life, in thirty years he would have planted so many more that these ten thousand would be like a drop of water in the ocean.

Besides, he was now studying the reproduction of beech trees and had a nursery of seedlings grown from beechnuts near his cottage. The seedlings, which he had protected from his sheep with a wire fence, were very beautiful. He was also considering birches for the valleys where, he told me, there was a certain amount of moisture a few yards below the surface of the soil.

The next day, we parted.

THE following year came the War of 1914, in which I was involved for the next five years. An infantryman hardly had time for reflecting upon trees. To tell the truth, the thing itself had made no impression upon me; I had considered it as a hobby, a stamp collection, and forgotten it.

The war over, I found myself possessed of a tiny demobilization bonus and a huge desire to breathe fresh air for a while. It was with no other objective that I again took the road to the barren lands.

The countryside had not changed. However, beyond the deserted village I glimpsed in the distance
a sort of greyish mist that covered the mountaintops
like a carpet. Since the day before, I had begun to
think again of the shepherd tree-planter. "Ten thousand oaks," I reflected, "really take up quite a bit of
space."

I had seen too many men die during those five
years not to imagine easily that Elzéard Bouffier was
dead, especially since, at twenty, one regards men
of fifty as old men with nothing left to do but die.

He was not dead. As a matter of fact, he was extremely spry. He had changed jobs. Now he had only four sheep but, instead, a hundred beehives. He had got rid of the sheep because they threatened his young trees. For, he told me (and I saw for myself), the war had disturbed him not at all. He had imperturbably continued to plant.

The oaks of 1910 were then ten years old and taller than either of us. It was an impressive spectacle. I was literally speechless and, as he did not talk, we spent the whole day walking in silence

through his forest. In three sections, it measured eleven kilometers in length and three kilometers at its greatest width. When you remembered that all this had sprung from the hands and the soul of this one man, without technical resources, you understood that men could be as effectual as God in other realms than that of destruction.

He had pursued his plan, and beech trees as high as my shoulder, spreading out as far as the eye could reach, confirmed it. He showed me handsome clumps of birch planted five years before—that is, in 1915, when I had been fighting at Verdun. He had set them out in all the valleys where he had guessed—and rightly—that there was moisture almost at the surface of the ground. They were as delicate as young girls, and very well established.

Creation seemed to come about in a sort of chain reaction. He did not worry about it; he was determinedly pursuing his task in all its simplicity; but as we went back toward the village I saw water flowing in brooks that had been dry since the memory of man. This was the most impressive result of chain reaction that I had seen. These dry streams had once, long ago, run with water. Some of the dreary villages

I mentioned before had been built on the sites of ancient Roman settlements, traces of which still remained; and archæologists, exploring there, had found fishhooks where, in the twentieth century, cisterns were needed to assure a small supply of water.

The wind, too, scattered seeds. As the water reappeared, so there reappeared willows, rushes, meadows, gardens, flowers, and a certain purpose in being alive. But the transformation took place so gradually that it became part of the pattern without causing any astonishment. Hunters, climbing into the wilderness in pursuit of hares or wild boar, had of course noticed the sudden growth of little trees, but had attributed it to some natural caprice of the earth. That is why no one meddled with Elzéard Bouffier's work. If he had been detected he would have had opposition. He was indetectable. Who in the villages or in the administration could have dreamed of such perseverance in a magnificent generosity?

To have anything like a precise idea of this exceptional character one must not forget that he worked in total solitude: so total that, toward the end of his life, he lost the habit of speech. Or perhaps it was that he saw no need for it.

IN 1933 he received a visit from a forest ranger who notified him of an order against lighting fires out of doors for fear of endangering the growth of this *natural* forest. It was the first time, the man told him naively, that he had ever heard of a forest growing of its own accord. At that time Bouffier was about to plant beeches at a spot some twelve kilometers from his cottage. In order to avoid travelling back and forth—for he was then seventy-five— he planned to build a stone cabin right at the plantation. The next year he did so.

In 1935 a whole delegation came from the Government to examine the "natural forest." There was a high official from the Forest Service, a deputy, technicians. There was a great deal of ineffectual talk. It was decided that something must be done and, fortunately, nothing was done except the only helpful thing: the whole forest was placed under the protection of the State, and charcoal burning prohibited. For it was impossible not to be captivated by the beauty of those young trees in the fulness of health, and they cast their spell over the deputy himself.

A friend of mine was among the forestry officers of the delegation. To him I explained the mystery. One day the following week we went together to see Elzéard Bouffier. We found him hard at work, some ten kilometers from the spot where the inspection had taken place.

This forester was not my friend for nothing. He was aware of values. He knew how to keep silent. I delivered the eggs I had brought as a present. We shared our lunch among the three of us and spent several hours in wordless contemplation of the countryside.

In the direction from which we had come the slopes were covered with trees twenty to twenty-five feet tall. I remembered how the land had looked in 1913: a desert . . . . Peaceful, regular toil, the vigorous mountain air, frugality and, above all, serenity of spirit had endowed this old man with awe-inspiring health. He was one of God's athletes. I wondered how many more acres he was going to cover with trees.

Before leaving, my friend simply made a brief suggestion about certain species of trees that the soil here seemed particularly suited for. He did not force the point. "For the very good reason," he told me later, "that Bouffier knows more about it than I do." At the end of an hour's walking—having turned it over in his mind—he added, "He knows a lot more about it than anybody. He's discovered a wonderful way to be happy!"

It was thanks to this officer that not only the forest but also the happiness of the man was protected. He delegated three rangers to the task, and so terrorized them that they remained proof against all the bottles of wine the charcoalburners could offer.

The only serious danger to the work occurred during the war of 1939. As cars were being run on gazogenes (wood-burning generators), there was never enough wood. Cutting was started among the oaks of 1910, but the area was so far from any railroads that the enterprise turned out to be financially unsound. It was abandoned. The shepherd had seen nothing of it. He was thirty kilometers away, peacefully continuing his work, ignoring the war of '39 as he had ignored that of '14.

I SAW Elzéard Bouffier for the last time in June of 1945. He was then eighty-seven. I had started back along the route through the wastelands; but now, in spite of the disorder in which the war had left the country, there was a bus running between the Durance Valley and the mountain. I attributed the fact that I no longer recognized the scenes of my earlier journeys to this relatively speedy transportation. It seemed to me, too, that the route took me through new territory. It took the name of a village to convince me that I was actually in that region that had been all ruins and desolation.

The bus put me down at Vergons. In 1913 this hamlet of ten or twelve houses had three inhabitants. They had been savage creatures, hating one another, living by trapping game, little removed, both physically and morally, from the conditions of prehistoric man. All about them nettles were feeding upon the remains of abandoned houses. Their condition had been beyond hope. For them, nothing but to await death—a situation which rarely predisposes to virtue.

Everything was changed. Even the air. Instead of the harsh dry winds that used to attack me, a gentle breeze was blowing, laden with scents. A sound like water came from the mountains: it was the wind in the forest. Most amazing of all, I heard the actual sound of water falling into a pool. I saw that a fountain had been built, that it flowed freely and—what touched me most—that someone had planted a linden beside it, a linden that must have been four years old, already in full leaf, the incontestable symbol of resurrection.

Besides, Vergons bore evidence of labor at the sort of undertaking for which hope is required. Hope, then, had returned. Ruins had been cleared away,

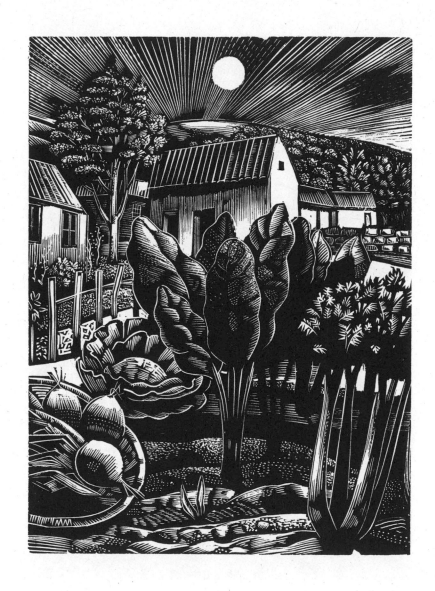

dilapidated walls torn down and five houses restored. Now there were twenty-eight inhabitants, four of them young married couples. The new houses, freshly plastered, were surrounded by gardens where vegetables and flowers grew in orderly confusion, cabbages and roses, leeks and snapdragons, celery and anemones. It was now a village where one would like to live.

From that point on I went on foot. The war just finished had not yet allowed the full blooming of life, but Lazarus was out of the tomb. On the lower slopes of the mountain I saw little fields of barley and of rye; deep in the narrow valleys the meadows were turning green.

It has taken only the eight years since then for the whole countryside to glow with health and prosperity. On the site of ruins I had seen in 1913 now stand neat farms, cleanly plastered, testifying to a happy and comfortable life. The old streams, fed by the rains and snows that the forest conserves, are flowing again. Their waters have been channeled. On each farm, in groves of maples, fountain pools over-

flow on to carpets of fresh mint. Little by little the villages have been rebuilt. People from the plains, where land is costly, have settled here, bringing youth, motion, the spirit of adventure. Along the roads you meet hearty men and women, boys and girls who understand laughter and have recovered a taste for picnics. Counting the former population, unrecognizable now that they live in comfort, more than ten thousand people owe their happiness to Elzéard Bouffier.

When I reflect that one man, armed only with his

own physical and moral resources, was able to cause this land of Canaan to spring from the wasteland, I am convinced that in spite of everything, humanity is admirable. But when I compute the unfailing greatness of spirit and the tenacity of benevolence that it must have taken to achieve this result, I am taken with an immense respect for that old and un-learned peasant who was able to complete a work worthy of God.

Elzéard Bouffier died peacefully in 1947 at the hospice in Banon.

AFTERWORD
to the original edition

I mustered enough courage to call upon Jean Giono in Manosque, Provence, at 11:00 A.M., August 15, 1970. His older daughter, Aline Giono, down from Paris for a few days, ushered me into the garden of their hillside home. Then dying from heart disease, Giono sat at a table, unable to walk any more, he told me at once. I could not believe his cultured voice, for I knew that he was self-taught. I have never recovered from the sight of him. He was positively stunning: slender, silver-haired, elegant, with delicate features, rosy cheeks, hooded blue eyes, casually dressed in tan slacks and mauve shirt. Without any hesitation he rushed into a dazzling discussion with me about books, critics, authors, Provence, his home, his life, his creativity. He begged me to stay and made me promise to return. I left that first day loaded down with gifts of his unpublished and privately published works, which I sent immediately to Butler Library, Columbia University. Less than two months later, Jean Giono died, midway through his seventy-fifth year.

Giono lived virtually his entire life in the little city of Manosque. His elderly father was a cobbler and his mother, he tells us in his early novel *Jean le bleu* (*Blue Boy*), ran a hand laundry. This family of three resided in the poorest of tenements where the child had only a blue view down into the well, or courtyard. At age sixteen, becoming sole support of the family, Giono left school and went to clerk in a bank. Eighteen years later, in 1929, he published his first two novels, *Colline* (*Hill of Destiny*) and *Un de Baumugnes* (*Lovers Are Never Losers*), both rave successes, in part thanks to the instant sponsorship of André Gide.

Years afterward Giono recalled the turning point in his life, that moment in the afternoon of December 20, 1911, when he could spare enough pennies to purchase the cheapest book he could find. It turned out to be a copy of Virgil's poems. He never forgot that first flush of his own creative energy: "My heart soared."

Giono laughingly said people in Paris sent him questionnaires because they did not want to read his books. But if we look at one of these documents he answered, we can hear him speak in his usual teasing voice and mood: My ideal of happiness? *Peace.* My favorite fictional hero? *Don Quixote.* My favorite historical character? *Machiavelli.* My heroines in real life? *There are no heroines in real life.* My painter? *Goya.* My musician? *Mozart.* My poet? *Villon. Baudelaire.* My color? *Red.* My flower? *The narcissus.* My chief character trait? *Generosity. Faithfulness.* My chief fault? *The generous lie.* What I want to be? *Lenient.* My preferred occupation? *Writing.*

* * *

Knowing his unique, exceptional, and, in fact, idiosyncratic patterns of thought, I am not surprised that Giono ran into difficulties with the American editors who in 1953 asked him to write a few pages about an unforgettable character. Apparently the publishers required a story about an actual unforgettable character, while Giono chose to write some pages about that character which to him *would be* most unforgettable. When what he wrote met with the objection that no "Bouffier" had died in the shelter at Banon, a tiny mountain hamlet, Giono donated his pages to all and sundry. Not long after the story was rejected, it was accepted by *Vogue* and published in March 1954 as "The Man Who Planted Hope and Grew Happiness." Giono later wrote an American admirer of the tale that his purpose in creating Bouffier "was to make people love the tree, or more precisely, to make them *love planting trees.*" Within a few years the story of Elzéard Bouffier swept around the world and was translated into at least a dozen languages. It has long since inspired reforestation efforts, worldwide.

We see from the opening sentence of the story how Giono interpreted the word "character," an individuality unforgettable if unselfish, generous beyond measure, leaving on earth its mark without thought or reward. Giono believed he left his mark on earth when he wrote Elzéard Bouffier's story because he gave it away for the good of others, heedless of payment: "it is one of my stories of which I am the proudest. It does not bring me in one single penny and that is why it has accomplished what it was written for."

In *The Man Who Planted Trees*, the author's adventure commenced in June 1913, during a walking tour through Julius Caesar's ancient Roman province, still so called: Provence. As Giono trudged along the wild, deserted high plateau, he heard the wind growl like a lion over the ruins which lay like black carcasses and rush like ocean waves over the high country. Fearful and exposed, he saw mirages like the gaunt, black silhouette of a grieving woman he mistook for a dead tree. He met a shepherd, a *pastor* ministering to sheep, one of those solitary men associated from all time with congregations and Providence. By the end of World War I this same shepherd had become a beekeeper who already resembled God more narrowly by his power to create a new earth. He was planting oaks, beeches, and birches. Miraculously, water was conserved, dry stream beds filled again, and seeds germinated into gardens, meadows, and flowers. In 1933 this planter of trees of seventy-five years of age was clearly one of God's athletes. After World War II the author saw new villages in Canaan, where in 1913 all had lain waste. The shepherd had performed his solitary work, which Giono hoped he also had done. Both hoped to be worthy of God.

The name Elzéard calls into mind some forgotten Hebrew prophet, wise man, or Oriental king. The last name means in both French and English something grandiose: *bouffi, bouffé,* that is, puffed up (like a great man), puffed out (like wind, or a cloud in the sky). Such an old hero appears remarkably in most of Giono's early fiction, often a shepherd, or else some venerable alcoholic, storyteller, old hired man, or knife sharpener, but usually escorted by beasts: sheep, bees, a bull, a stag, a toad, or a serpent. Such lonely old men in their delirium directly hear the voice of God, or that of some ageless Greek divinity such as the great Pan. One must think of these variously gifted old men as embodying the creative gods themselves, as native survivals in this ancient Provence to which they continuously brought their wisdom, their knowledge of agriculture, their message of life indestructible, all of them teaching, like the titanic Dionysus, the precious secret of humanity's ancient kinship with the earth.

From the 1920s Giono continually praised this harmony whereby human beings conserved and enriched the earth where they coexisted with animals, both enriched by the silent but responsive, living vegetable kingdom. Giono also praised work done in solitude, where creation originates and, especially in humankind, where the free expression of compassion and pity begins.

When we express pity, Giono used to say, as for a living river cut off by dams, or pity for the helpless, suffering beast killed by cruel humankind, then we ourselves resemble the ancient yellow gods who still look down on us from Olympus. Should we not extend our compassion to the forest before it is felled by the woodcutters? This was not original in French literature, of course, but could have come to the child Giono as he read the *Fables* of La Fontaine in school. His thinking was reinforced by his favorite American "apostles of Nature," Walt Whitman and Henry David Thoreau.

We are probably accustomed to regional authors who express their love for animals and who encourage us to treat them with kindness and respect. Giono aside, we are less used to those writers who look upon the plant kingdom as coequal with the animal kingdom. We have begun to recognize a new fellowship with the silent vegetable world, because it purifies and renews the earth about us, because it comforts us, and because it reconciles us to death.

In *Solitude de la pitié* (1932) Giono illustrates all of

this by telling us a whole series of tragi-comical stories. Once upon a time there was, he tell us, a feeble old country fellow named Jofroi, who sold his peach orchard to his neighbor Fonse in order to purchase an annuity for himself and his flustered old wife Barbe. Fine, until the day Fonse decided that the peach trees were diseased and old, and furthermore decided to cut them down. Then, in utter despair, Jofroi set about attempting to take his own life, but was always frustrated by Barbe. Jofroi never could stop explaining to anyone who would listen that these were his own trees, which he had planted, and watered by hand, and still owned. And owned forever.

In another tale from this collection, a tale I think of in English as "In the Woodcutters' Country," Giono tells how a young shepherd one day came to call on his friend Firmin, way up in the isolated hill country. The two friends finally could not stand to hear Firmin's wife crying in labor. So they walked all the way down into the valley, uprooted a large cypress, and lugged it back up the hill to home. They planted it by the front door where Madelon could hear it singing in the wind. Her baby was christened in its shade. The tree burbled in the dry wind storms like a stream of water in heaven. Firmin passed on. Madelon too. The boy never came back from war. The tree is still there.

In his wonderful story of Elzéard Bouffier, Giono frankly seems to have intended to inspire a reforestation program that would renew the whole earth. His history of this imaginary shepherd, which is a compliment to Americans because of its relationship to the real Johnny

Appleseed, calmly veers away from past and present time toward the future of newer and better generations. Giono termed his confidence in the future *espérance*, or hopefulness, not *espoir*, which is the masculine word for hope, but *espérance*, the feminine word designating the permanent state or condition of living one's life in hopeful tranquility. Whence springs this well of *espérance*, Giono wondered?

Hopefulness must spring, he decided, from literature and the profession of poetry. Authors only write. So, to be fair about it, they have an obligation to profess hopefulness, in return for their right to live and write. The poet must know the magical effect of certain words: hay, grass, meadows, willows, rivers, firs, mountains, hills. People have suffered so long inside the walls that they have forgotten to be free, Giono thought. Human beings were not created to live forever in subways and tenements, for their feet long to stride through tall grass, or slide though running water. The poet's mission is to remind us of beauty, of trees swaying in the breeze, or pines groaning under snow in the mountain passes, of wild white horses galloping across the surf.

You know, Giono said to me, there are also times in life when a person has to rush off in pursuit of hopefulness.

* * *

During his lifetime Jean Giono, who considered himself to be Italian and Provençal, in addition to French, was judged one of the greatest writers of our age by such authorities as Henri Peyre and André Malraux. Both Peyre and Malraux ranked Giono first or second in

French twentieth century literature: Giono, Montherlant, and Malraux (who included himself). Longevity counts most for an author, and Giono's works are still being edited and published after fifty-six years. Giono wrote over thirty novels, numerous essays, scores of stories, many of which were published as collections, plays, and film scripts. In 1953 he was awarded the Prix Monégasque for his collective work, and in 1954 he was elected to Académie Goncourt, whose ten members award the annual Prix Goncourt.

In recent years some of Giono's most highly regarded novels have been reprinted by North Point Press and are once again available to English-speaking readers. These are: *Harvest* (1930), *Blue Boy* (1932), *Song of the World* (1934), *Joy of Man's Desiring* (1935), *Horseman of the Roof* (1951), and *The Straw Man* (1958).

Norma L. Goodrich
Claremont, California
May 1985

Norma L. Goodrich, a native Vermonter, has spent many years in France and is intimately familiar with Provence. After heading a private school in France during the 1950s, she returned to the United States and earned a Ph.D. in French literature at Columbia University. For the last twenty years she has lived in California and is presently Professor Emeritus of French and Comparative Literature at the Claremont Colleges. She is author of numerous scholarly works, including *Giono: Master of Fictional Modes*.

AFTERWORD
to the twentieth anniversary edition

Trees Are Our Partners

Having spent the last thirty-five years planting trees in pursuit of an environmental restoration akin in spirit to Jean Giono's, I find the story a refreshing and re-inspiring reminder of the long-term payoff of my work. The story is beautiful in its simplicity. It speaks to the promise of tree planting and its power to restore health, abundance, community, water, habitat, and life itself. I believe it touches on archetypal ideas that we all carry, imprinted somewhere in our genes, about our human need to work with trees to repair and restore the life-support systems of our damaged planet.

The effects of tree planting can be profound for reversing the current environmental decline in cities and rural areas across the globe. The need for people to participate in urban and rural forestry efforts has never been greater. Climate change, desertification, drinking water shortages, urban flooding, storm-water pollution, skin cancer, and pollution-caused lung disease are worsening and increasingly threatening human health and safety and economic opportunity throughout the world. Tree planting and community forestry provide some of the most effective tools to prevent or mitigate these immense problems.

Because tree planting is potentially so powerful and because the global need is so great, it is important for readers to understand both the challenges and possibilities so that they can take effective action, whether they get involved by supporting others or make their own commitments.

The Story of TreePeople

My own story of starting TreePeople illustrates what is possible. Growing up in Los Angeles, I developed a special relationship with the mountain forests about two hours east of the city. My parents used to send me to the San Bernardino Mountains for summer camp, and there I grew to love the forest, in part because tree-cleansed fresh air provided a respite from the city's lung-stinging pollution. In 1970, when I turned fifteen, the U.S. Forest Service announced that the trees and forest were being killed by air pollution and declared that if nothing was done, the local forest as we knew it would be dead by the year 2000. Under the direction of camp leaders, I worked with other teenagers for three weeks planting a meadow and grove of smog-tolerant trees on an area that had been turned into a truck parking lot. That work felt so good that I wanted to keep going and get kids all over the forest to plant trees and work to save it.

After three years of trying, failing, quitting, learning, and trying again, I finally succeeded in rounding up

8,000 trees, tools, trucks, and a crew of camp and college friends. A news article in the *Los Angeles Times* inspired thousands of people to send donations of fifty cents to a dollar apiece, and so with a tiny budget, and help from my family, we incorporated as a nonprofit organization and launched TreePeople. We spent the first summer teaching campers throughout the San Bernadino forest about why it was dying and why they were needed to save it. Then we worked with them to plant the trees and water them.

The summer planting quickly grew into an annual effort. We realized that because smog from the city was killing the trees, we needed to clean up the city air to protect the forest trees. With some of the worst air in the United States, and little interest or progress in cleaning it up at that time, I sought to involve city people in the hope that their participation would deepen their awareness and motivate them to take care of the air and the environment, and that they would become willing to make the lifestyle changes needed to get there. We launched environmental education and urban forestry programs, involving thousands of school children and their families in planting trees in both the city and the mountain forests.

The programs grew in their reach and sophistication. We launched a four-year campaign to inform and motivate the people of greater Los Angeles to plant one million trees before the 1984 Summer Olympic Games. Learning of the planned destruction of nearly one million surplus fruit trees, we organized to rescue, prune, prepare, and distribute tens of thousands of them to thousands of low-income families. Those trees survived to produce tons of fruit along with lessons and hope for the families who cared for them. Several years later, when we learned of the sub-Saharan famine, we partnered with international nongovernmental organizations (NGOs) and local organizations in fourteen villages in four countries in Africa. Two TreePeople volunteers worked with each village to prepare the people and sites for the trees, and when each region was ready, we put prepared trees on Pan Am jets and airlifted them over for planting. After six months, villagers and volunteers had planted five thousand large trees in Ethiopia, Kenya, Tanzania, and the Cameroon.

Although our plantings were very successful, it took many years of trial and error to learn that the benefits of trees are not guaranteed by random acts of planting. We also learned that without proper planning, site, and tree selection, it was possible to worsen all of these issues while wasting precious time and money.

These important lessons ultimately shaped our organization into a vehicle poised to transform Los Angeles into a sustainable urban environment. In three decades we went through three distinct phases. I share these stages to help others avoid having to reinvent the wheel.

During the first ten years, although we were a grassroots organization, we planted trees *for* people. We perfected the mechanism of recruiting and training volunteers and ensuring that trees were planted well. But in evaluating long-term impacts, we found that tree survival wasn't as high as we'd hoped because the neighborhood people weren't taking care of and protecting the trees; they didn't feel they *owned* the trees.

We focused our second decade on teaching, guiding and supporting people to become Citizen Foresters. With an in-depth training and support program, ordinary people learned how to make their dreams manifest in their own neighborhoods. They organized their neighborhoods, raised some funds, and hosted the plantings, ensuring a profound sense of ownership. We backed them up with tools, trucks, insurance, and from dozens to hundreds of volunteers, depending on their needs. The result: we found that 90 percent of Citizen Forester–planted trees were alive after five years, combating the U.S. average national life span of seven years for urban trees.

After twenty years, I began to wonder if our trees were making enough of a difference to counter all the damage our city was doing to human health and the world's environment. They weren't. So I launched a ten-year, million dollar research effort called the T.R.E.E.S. Project (Trans-agency Resources for Environmental and Economic Sustainability) and learned that trees could have a tremendous impact if we applied the best practices of science, forestry, engineering, and watershed management. But to accomplish our goals, we needed to shift from random planting to strategic planting. We needed to begin practicing the *acupuncture* of planting, very consciously selecting and placing trees so they could capture, clean, and retain rainfall, while preventing pollution, drought, and flooding. We also needed to plant trees so that they could conserve energy and prevent air pollution by shading buildings, parking lots, and parked cars. Finally, we needed to mulch the fallen leaves and pruned branches to capture and recycle the nutrients, to conserve water, and to reduce the urban waste stream (40 percent of which is green "waste" in Los Angeles). All of this can happen by choosing the right tree for the right place, and by redesigning and adapting city land—with trees and tree-mimicking technologies like cisterns—to function like a forest.

That research paid off big time for the trees. While most government agencies and people appreciate trees, public investment in tree planting and maintenance values them only as decorations. When budgets are tight, tree maintenance and planting funds are nearly always among the first to be cut. We showed that it is technically and economically feasible for trees to solve key urban issues. Since we demonstrated trees' strategic value, several key government agencies have dramatically altered their names, missions, programs, and budgets to incorporate trees and urban watersheds to solve problems. In Sun Valley, a Los Angeles suburb, the County Public Works Department's new Watershed Management Division (formerly Flood Control) is developing a $200 million urban watershed plan instead of building a $50 million concrete storm drain. The higher cost is justified because the watershed approach will more than pay for itself in conserved water and energy and avoided pollution.

The Los Angeles experience is now being replicated in other cities around the United States. With proper research, planning, design, education, and public involvement, these profound changes are possible and applicable in cities around the world.

All of this grew out of the simple tree-planting action and dreams of one teenager. But these dreams have only taken root because thousands of people believed in and generously supported them, hundreds of others (over the years) joined his staff, thousands volunteered their time and energy, and then dozens of government agencies and other NGOs partnered, tested, improved, and implemented the ideas. And the story continues to unfold. Please check the TreePeople Web site (www.treepeople.org) for updates, newsletters, and more information—or to support our work.

How Trees Help Today

In addition to restoring soil structure and fertility, watershed functionality, and habitat to rural lands, trees are among the best tools we have for combating some of the world's most pressing environmental problems.

On the most basic level, trees protect people's lives. Consider the tsunami that struck the Indian Ocean just after Christmas 2004. As of the time of this writing, nearly 300,000 people in 12 countries were killed by the wave that followed a massive earthquake. Villages and towns thousands of miles away from the quake's epicenter were devastated by the power of the water—except for the very few locations where natural mangrove forests were still intact. Mangrove forests are dense and grow along the shoreline and in coastal waters off tropical and semi-tropical land. They protect the land and the people by absorbing the force of a wave as it hits. According to early reports, far fewer people died and the areas behind the mangroves suffered far less damage. Unfortunately, in most of the populated regions around the Indian Ocean, the mangroves have been cut down to make way for development and shrimp farms. Research will tell whether a massive mangrove forest restoration effort is needed to better protect the millions of people who live in tropical lowlands adjacent to coastal waters.

Trees are just as important in developed countries. Trees and forests, both urban and rural, are models of sustainability. They help reduce air pollution and global warming gases; water pollution, drought, and flooding; energy use through conservation; and waste (e.g., mulching garden waste), while improving human physical and psychological health and the economy. Through careful and well-planned planting and restoration, it is possible to establish urban and rural forests that cost-effectively replace and enhance these natural life-support services, which are being lost to development and sprawl.

Scientists report that nearly every natural ecosystem across the planet is showing signs of human-caused stress, and many are being wiped out entirely by urbanization and pollution. The consequences are significant.

What You Can Do

Sometimes doing the work of tree-planting and ecological restoration can seem like swimming against the tide. Be ready for problems and setbacks, and greet them as interesting challenges and lessons to strengthen you and your vision. In Western society we've grown to view problems as signs of failure, but this notion is disempowering. Because I spent so many years at the beginning trying and failing—

and ultimately learning extremely valuable lessons—I came to view problems as gifts. Their solutions always provide extra energy (answers, friends, funds) to carry projects further toward their goals. I also came to view mistakes, not as failures, but as compost for success, rich in information needed to nourish future efforts.

Whether you want to plant a single tree or restore an entire watershed, there is information to guide you so that your efforts succeed. Whether you are an individual, a family, an existing organization, or a city, there are resources available to guide your planning, planting, and long-term care.

Andy Lipkis
Founder and President
TreePeople, Los Angeles, California
February 2005

RESOURCES

First Steps

Here are a few key thoughts to consider if you want to take action:

Know that you absolutely can and do make a difference.

Take small steps first that you can easily sustain. Plant one or two trees to learn what's involved and how much energy it takes.

Be prepared to commit some time. We say it takes five years to plant a tree, meaning the time required to plan, plant, and take care of it till it is established.

Don't reinvent the wheel. Look for other people or organizations that are already working in your area and see if you can join or support their efforts. Find out what they need most and see if you can fit in.

Find guidance for your local ecology and climate; every area has very different conditions that dictate appropriate species and planting techniques. Use the resources listed below, or try contacting a local nursery, botanical garden, library, forester, extension agent, university, or garden club.

The Simple Act of Planting A Tree

In response to the thousands of people from around the world who turned to TreePeople seeking guidance, my wife and partner, Katie, and I wrote a guidebook that enables you to develop any idea into a successful project. *The Simple Act of Planting a Tree: A Citizen Foresters' Guide to Healing Your Neighborhood, Your City and Your World* takes you through every essential step from dreaming through project execution. It helps you to site and choose the right tree for the right place and provides instructions and illustrations on proper planting, care, and pruning techniques.

Even more potent for larger efforts, the book can help you develop an idea or dream, find like-minded supporters, develop a plan, raise funds, get government permits, recruit and train volunteers, acquire needed equipment, organize community meetings, get publicity, plant your trees, and organize follow-up care and ongoing activities.

The book is available from TreePeople (www.treepeople.org). There is an online version at www.treepeople.org/simpleact.

Assistance on All Levels

Because tree planting is so important, both nongovernmental and government organizations and networks have been set up throughout the United States (and most countries) to support local efforts. There is a State Forester, an Urban Forestry Coordinator, and a Volunteer

Coordinator in every state of the United States. The United Kingdom has the National Urban Forestry Unit and a network of Community Forests in place to guide and organize local action. In Australia, the organization Land Care has deployed local units throughout the country. Back in the United States, there are statewide and regional nongovernmental organizations. Please see the following list to get started, and visit TreeLink at www.treelink.org for a complete, up-to-date directory of national, international, regional, state, and local organizations and resources.

Andy Lipkis

U.S. Organizations

American Forests
P.O. Box 2000
Washington, DC 20013
Telephone: 202-955-4500
Fax: 202-955-4588
E-mail: info@amfor.org
Web site: www.americanforests.org

National Alliance for Community Trees
4302 Baltimore Ave.
Bladensburg, MD 20710-1031
Telephone: 301-699-8635
Fax: 301-699-3317
Web site: www.actrees.org

National Arbor Day Foundation
100 Arbor Avenue
Nebraska City, NE 68410
Telephone: 888-448-7337
Web site: www.arborday.com

National Tree Trust
1120 G Street, NW
Suite 770
Washington, DC 20005
Telephone: 800-846-TREE (8733)
          202-628-8733 (within Washington, DC)
Fax: 202-628-8735
Web site: www.nationaltreetrust.org

National Urban and Community Forestry
  Advisory Council
USDA Forest Service
P.O. Box 1003
Sugarloaf, CA 92386-1003
Telephone: 909-585-9268
Fax: 909-585-9527
Web site: www.treelink.org/nucfac

TreePeople
12601 Mulholland Drive
Beverly Hills, CA 90210
Telephone: 818-753-4600
Fax: 818-753-4635
E-mail: info@treepeople.org
Web site: www.treepeople.org

Trees for Life
3006 W. St. Louis
Wichita, KS 67203-5129
Telephone: 316-945-6929
Fax: 316-945-0909
E-mail: info@treesforlife.org
Web site: www.treesforlife.org
This U.S.-based organization helps people plant fruit trees in developing countries.

International Organizations

**European Urban Forestry Research and
  Information Centre (EUFORIC)**
Jasper Schipperijn
EUFORIC Coordinator
Danish Center for Forest, Landscape, and Planning
The Royal Veterinary and Agriculture University
Rolighedsvej 23, DK-1958 Frederiksberg C
Denmark
Telephone: (+45) 3258-1780
Fax: (+45) 3528-1508
Web site: www.sl.kvl.dk/euforic/index.htm

The Green Belt Movement
P.O. Box 67545
Nairobi, Kenya
Africa
Telephone: (+254) 20-573057
          (+254) 20-571523
E-mail: gbm@wananchi.com
Web site: www.greenbeltmovement.org

Tree Canada Foundation
220 Laurier Avenue West, Suite 750
Ottawa, Ontario K1P 5Z9
Canada
Telephone: 613-567-5545
Fax: 613-567-5270
E-mail: tcf@treecanada.ca
Web site: www.treecanada.ca

The Woodland Trust
Autumn Park
Dysart Road
Grantham
Lincolnshire NG31 6LL
United Kingdom
Telephone: (+01) 476-581111
Fax: (+01) 476-590808
Web site: www.woodland-trust.org.uk

This short list was compiled with the assistance of Pepper Provenzano, founder and director of TreeLink. Please visit www.treelink.org for a complete list of tree-planting and conservation organizations at all levels— local, state, regional, national, and international. TreeLink also maintains a variety of frequently updated online resources for groups and individuals.

The Man Who Planted Trees was designed, set in Times Roman, and illustrated by Michael McCurdy. This twentieth anniversary edition has been printed and bound by Friesens, on sixty-pound Rolland Enviro Edition 100, a chlorine-free paper made from 100 percent post-consumer recycled fibers.

Jean Giono (1895–1970), the only son of a cobbler and a laundress, was one of France's greatest writers. He was a pacifist, and he was imprisoned in France for his beliefs during the Second World War. He wrote over thirty novels, scores of short stories, plays, poetry, essays, and film-scripts. Giono won the Prix de Monaco (for the most outstanding collected work by a French writer) among other awards.

Michael McCurdy is one of America's finest wood engravers. He has illustrated nearly 200 books for trade publications and special fine-press editions. He lives in Springfield, Massachusetts.

Wangari Maathai is the 2004 Nobel Peace Prize laureate, founder of the Green Belt Movement, and author of the book *The Green Belt Movement: Sharing the Approach and the Experience* (Lantern Books, 2003).

Andy Lipkis is the founder and president of TreePeople in Los Angeles, California.

CHELSEA GREEN
PUBLISHING

the politics and practice of sustainable living

Shelter

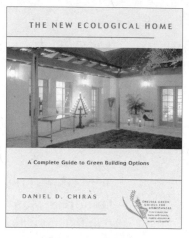

Planet

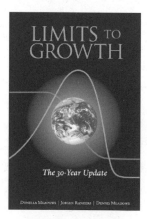

People

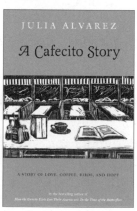

Food